PEPPERS DAY OUT!

OPCORN

Lena R. Williams

To order additional copies of this book, contact:
Xlibris
844-714-8691
www.Xlibris.com
Orders@Xlibris.com

ISBN: Softcover   978-1-6641-8818-1
       EBook   978-1-6641-8817-4

Library of Congress Control Number: 2021916612

Print information available on the last page.

Rev. date: 08/25/2021

PEPPER'S DAY OUT!

Once upon a time there was a little poodle named Pepper, who lived in the big city in an apartment with her owner and the family cat, Sidney. She never went outside by herself without her owner on a leash, her owner loved her very much and Pepper was a very happy dog who brought joy to her owner. One day she left for work and left her alone, she told Pepper that the repair man would come by to fix some things and not to worry and to behave themselves, and that Sidney would be there to keep her company.

Once the repair man got there, he left the front door to the home ajar and Pepper nudged it open and ventured out into the world. Once outside Pepper was amazed at how big the world was, "wow" she said excitedly, happy about being outside on her own, she wanted to explore this amazing world alone, so she ventured to the curb of the street to see the pretty colors of the cars that zoomed by and—kerplunk! an acorn hit her on her head.

"Ouch!" she yelped, looking up at the furry little creature laughing loudly. "What's so funny?!" she asked, (rubbing her head where the acorn hit) "You are, kid!" the squirrel said, "don't you know those things are dangerous?" "No." she replied, "at least they are not when I am riding in them." She said. "Well" said the squirrel, "That's the thing, you are *in* them, not under them!" The squirrel laughed. Well, I did not know that, I've never been out on my own before" Pepper said, amazed.

"Aren't you Pepper?" the squirrel asked, "yes" Pepper replied, "how'd you know?" The squirrel replied "well, I see you all the time with your owner on your leash, I thought you looked familiar, what are you doing out by yourself?"

Pepper said, "Well, my owner said she was going to work, and she'd be back, and that the repair guy would be there in a while, and Sidney would keep me company, then the repair guy left the door cracked and I came out and here I am!"

"Oh, that's interesting" the squirrel said, "look kid, it's a big world, why don't you stick with me until your owner gets back?" Pepper said, "I don't know you, what's your name?" "Scooter" the squirrel said proudly, "Scooter the squirrel, at your service!" "Look, I am going to the circus, you want to tag along?"

"Sure!" Pepper said excitedly, "But what's a circus?"

"It's an event with a big tent with animals, games and fun!" the squirrel said, "You'll love it!"

"Ok." Pepper agreed, then she asked the squirrel "well, how do we get there?" The squirrel replied, "That's the thing about us squirrels, we know lots of shortcuts!"

So, Scooter and Pepper took a few shortcuts through people's backyards on their way to the circus, along the way, Pepper realized "I've never been out on my own before, it's exciting and scary all at once" The squirrel said "well, I can see that, you are a house pet, you don't have to worry about anything, you got it made in the shade!"

"Not really.", Pepper replied. "I have this brother, Sidney, he's a cat, he gets on my nerves!" "Oh, cats, us squirrels have to be weary of them out here, they'll get us, what color is he?" Scooter asked.

"Orange." Pepper said," but you don't have to worry, he's a housecat, he never goes outside."

"Oh, that's a relief!" Scooter replied. As our friends neared the circus, they were taken aback by the sights and sounds abound at the circus, the trumpet of the elephants, the roar of the lions and tigers, the smells of the snacks and treats being served. "Hmm, that smells good!" Pepper said, sniffing the air, "what is it?"

"Oh, that's popcorn" Scooter said, sniffing as well, "I wonder where it's coming from?"

"Pepper replied "over there!" pointing toward the concession stand, and her and Scooter scurried over quickly, upon getting to the stand a loud voice says, "Hold it, who says you can come over here?!"

Pepper raised her head up only to see the scary image of a big German Shepherd, "Well?!" the Shepherd said, eyes staring at Pepper. "Well, I'm Pepper, and this here is my friend, Scooter, we smelled the popcorn and it smelled so good that we had to get some" Pepper explained.

"Well, who said you can get some?", This here is *our* stand, go find your own!"

"Pepper tilted her head, puzzled, "Our?", "There's only one of you!" she said.

"Is that right?" said the German shepherd, chuckling softly, giving a signal, Pepper suddenly is lifted in the air.

"Put me down! Put me down!" Pepper yelped, as she turned around, attempting to swing her paws at who was holding her, a Bulldog says, "My, we have a feisty one, don't we?"

"Alright guys, you've had your fun" a third dog says, "Come on, Colleen, we were just joking around!" says the Bulldog, laughing.

"I know, fun's over" said the Collie, so the bulldog put Pepper back down. "Thank you!" Pepper said thankfully, shaking herself off, "what's your name?" Pepper asked.

"Well, I'm Colleen, she explained, that is Billy, pointing to the -Bulldog, and next to me is Max, the German Shepherd. "What's your name? "Colleen asked. "My name is Pepper, she replied.

"Where are you guy's owners? Pepper asked, the other dogs looked puzzled, "owners?!" Max said, "We don't have owners kid, my friends and I are strays!"

"What's a stray?" Pepper asked bewildered, Max said "Well, a stray is a homeless dog, kid." "Homeless?!" Pepper said with a sad face, "that's so sad!", "What's so sad about being a stray?" Billy exclaimed, "It's the best!", "Yeah", Max said in agreement, "being a stray is the coolest, you have freedom, *real* freedom, and you don't have to depend on humans to walk you, you eat the best food, human food, we see the world, it's great!"

"Wow!" said Pepper, it does sound pretty cool, Scooter tells Pepper, "don't believe that Pepper, you have a good life at home and an owner that loves you!"

Pepper says, "I'm not thinking of becoming a stray silly, I was just thinking that it sounds cool is all."

"What's so cool about it?" Scooter says, "It's not so great in the winter time is it?" "Also, what about days you don't find anything to eat, is it so great then? "Scooter protesting what he thinks, Pepper is considering becoming a stray dog.

"Small potatoes" Max said, "There are not so great days, but overall, I would not trade it to be a stinking house dog!" Max said convincingly.

"True" Colleen explained, "There are rough patches here and there, but we stray dogs are tough, we are survivors." Colleen said, proudly. "But we'll let you have some popcorn since you did not know, ok?"

"Oh, thank you!" Pepper said excitedly, munching hungrily, "Scooter, and I have come a long way and we are starving!" she said. "Go right ahead!" Colleen told Pepper, "There is plenty for all of us!"

"Are you going to the Big Tent?" Colleen asked Pepper and Scooter. Scooter replied, "Yeah, that's what I brought Pep here to show her, she's never been out the house by herself alone before."

"Well, there is a first time for everything" Max said, with the other dogs nodding in agreement. "Come on, we're going to miss the main attraction!"

As Pepper, Scooter and their newfound friends make their way to the big tent, they hear the ring announcer start the show, trumpets and fanfare begin, the dogs find themselves a small opening in the tent and watch the show from under the bleachers.

"This is great Scoot, thanks for bringing me" Pepper said.

"I come all the time Pepper, it's no problem at all!" Scooter replied.

"Shhh!" Will you two keep it down?!" Colleen and Max asked the talkative twosome.

"Oh, Ok!" Scooter and Pepper said, and continued watching the main attraction in amazement. Tigers jumping through fire hoops, Elephants on stools, Seals balancing balls on their noses, Fire twirlers and Trapeze artists and tightrope walkers.

After a few hours had gone by, Pepper looked and saw that it was starting to get dark outside.

"Hey, my owner will be home soon!" Pepper said in shock, "I can't believe how fast the time flew!" "How will I get home in time?"

"See?" Billy said, "now you have to be home to meet your owner, what dog in their right mind would want to live like that?!"

"Quiet, Billy" Colleen, said, with a stern look on her face, looking as if she's thinking how to fix this. "We'll all take Pepper home, she and Scooter will ride on Max's back, he's the fastest, the rest of us will follow." Colleen says.

So, Pepper and Scooter climbed on Max's back while Max told them to hold on tight, then Max started into a steady jog.

"This is first class, huh?" Scooter laughed. "On the back of another dog is the only way to travel!"

"You bet!" Pepper said, "now if we can get him not to be so bumpy!"

"Max replied, "Hey, beggars can't be choosy! now enjoy the ride."

Soon enough, Pepper, Scooter and their friends were back at Pepper's home dropping her off and saying their goodbyes.

"Ok Pepper, now you take care of yourself kid, and don't be a stranger, we'll see you on the flipside!" Billy, Colleen and Max said.

"Where are you guys going?" Pepper said. Colleen replied, "to see the world, we have to catch a train later on tonight!"

"Hey Pep, how are you going to get in?" Max asked. Pepper replied "well, my "brother"" Sidney is in there, he'll open up the window for me."

"Is he a dog?" Billy asked, "Where is this Sidney?" Billy says, peering in the window with paws on the glass.

"Well, not quite guys, he's a cat" Pepper explained.

"A CAT?!!" the group said in shock, "well, how's he your brother? They asked.

"Well, he's not really my brother, my owner just calls him that because he lives in the house too!"

"Ok, that's cool!" Colleen and the other dogs said, "Now where is this Sidney?"

Pepper said, "He's usually in the window sunbathing or something, I'll knock on the window."

Pepper goes and knocks on the window a few times and Sidney jumps up into the window and replies "What the heck do *you* want?"

"Let me in!" Pepper barked hastily, "Where the heck have you been?!" Sidney replied, "I've been out" Pepper replied, "I went to the circus and had lots of fun!" *Yes* I can see that, you know it would be delightful to just... *leave* you out there and let our owner find you out there, wouldn't it?" Sidney said in a calm, serene way, "You'd be in lots of trouble!"

"Oh, no" Pepper said scared, "Sidney please don't do that, I'll do whatever you want for the next week, ok?" "Two!" Sidney replied, stroking his whiskers mischievously. "It's a Deal!" Pepper said, shaking her head in agreement.

Sidney unlocks the window latch and raises the window up to let Pepper in. Upon opening the window, Max snatches Sidney out of the window.

"What's your problem?! Max growled angrily, "Nothing, nothing at all!" Sidney chuckled nervously, "I was just giving Pepper the run-around, it's our way of showing affection!" Sidney gulped, "She knows I was going to let her in!" "We do it all the time, right Pepper?" Sidney, with a pleading look on his face.

Pepper, wanting to be nice and let Sidney off the hook slowly agrees "Yeah, we do it all the time Max, he's cool" Pepper says.

"Well, it'd better be, because if I hear you giving Pepper a hard time, you are going to have to deal with me, okay?!" Max said sternly, putting Sidney down.

"I totally understand!" Sidney says, nodding his head quickly.

"Can we go now? it's getting dark!" the other dogs and Scooter moaned in protest, "We have to hurry up if we are going to catch this freight train!"

"Alright" Max said, putting Sidney back inside the house and giving Pepper a boost into the window.

"Ok, Kid!" Max said happily, "We'll see you around!" Max said as he and the other dogs scurried off "and we'll look you up if we're ever back in town ok?

"Ok!" Pepper barked happily, her and Sidney put the window down and jumped out of the window sill.

"Whew, that was a close one!" Pepper said, "Thanks Sidney for letting me in!"

"No problem Pep." Sidney meowed as he hopped back into his bed, as Pepper pranced her way to hers, she heard door-keys jingling in the door, as she placed her eyes upon her beloved owner coming through the door.

"Yay!" Pepper excited, running happily to her and jumping into her arms, Pepper began to tell her owner about her day.

"And I went to the circus, I had popcorn, I saw Tigers, Elephants, Fire twirlers, and everything!" Pepper barked at her owner.

And her owner replied, "What are you barking about?!" "What do you want, a treat?!" "To go outside or what?!" "What are you trying to tell me Pepper?!" Her owner said, chuckling.

"And Pepper, you smell like a circus, I am going to give you a bath right away!"

THE END!

Williams, L. (2010). *Pepper's day out!*